Can I Bring My Pterodactyl to School, Ms. Johnson?

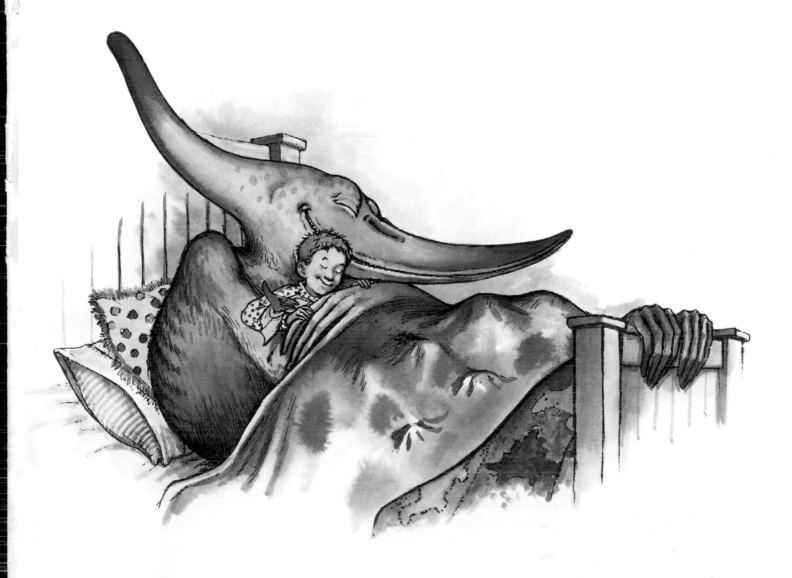

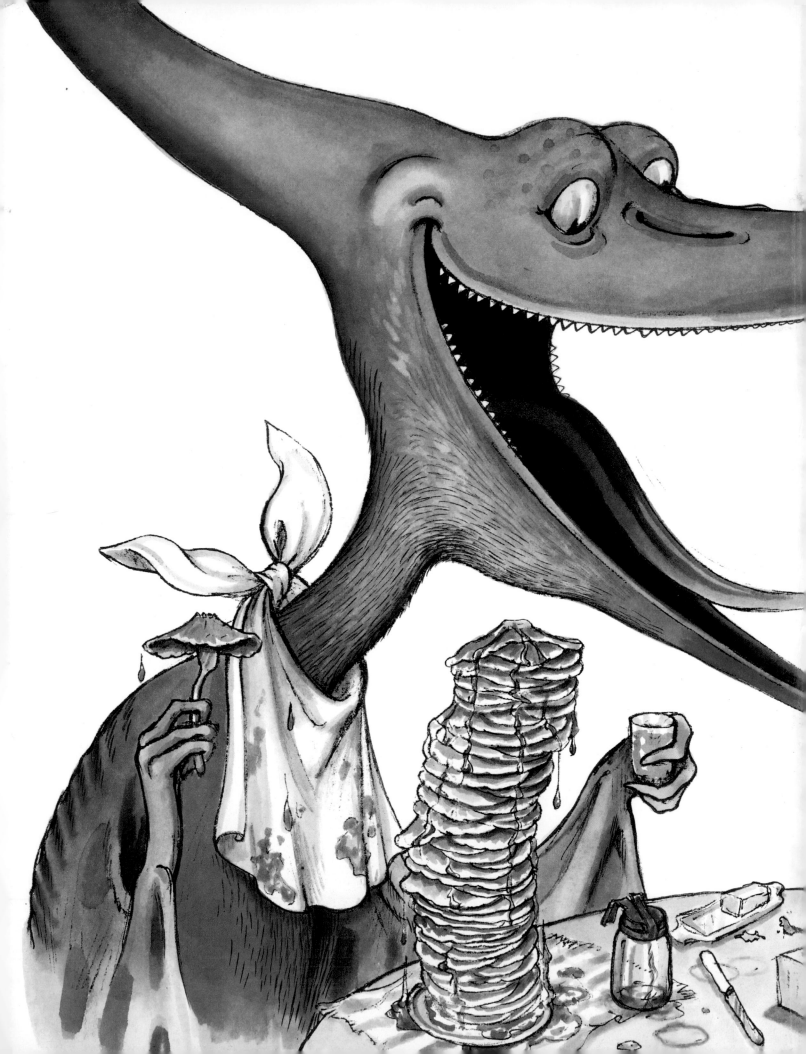

Can I Bring My Pterodactyl to School, Ms. Johnson?

Lois G. Grambling

Illustrated by
Judy Love

Charlesbridge

To eight super Gramblings chronologically listed,
Art, Jeff, Mark, Marcia, Lara, Ty, Mason, and Jesse.
And to Randi, who hung in there and helped me
make everything better.

—L. G. G.

To Tom—who has become so much more than
a little brown bat—with thanks for your insightful
criticism, your gentle encouragement, and your
boundless love.

—J. L.

Text copyright © 2006 by Lois G. Grambling
Illustrations copyright © 2006 by Judy Love

Published by Charlesbridge
85 Main Street
Watertown, MA 02472
(617) 926-0329
www.charlesbridge.com

Library of Congress Cataloging-in-Publication Data
Grambling, Lois G.
    Can I bring my pterodactyl to school, Ms. Johnson? / Lois G. Grambling ;
illustrated by Judy Love.
        p. cm.
    Summary: A child offers many creative reasons for why it would be a good
idea to bring a pterodactyl to school.
    ISBN-13: 978-1-58089-044-1; ISBN-10: 1-58089-044-X (reinforced for library use)
    ISBN-13: 978-1-58089-141-7; ISBN-10: 1-58089-141-1 (softcover)
[1. Pterodactyls—Fiction. 2. Dinosaurs—Fiction. 3. Schools—Fiction.]
I. Love, Judith DuFour, ill. II. Title.
PZ7.G7655   Cab 2006
[E]—dc22   2005005345

Printed in China
(hc) 10 9 8 7 6 5 4 3 2
(sc) 10 9 8 7 6 5 4 3

Illustrations done in transparent dyes on Strathmore paper
Display type and text type set in Big Limbo and Tempus Sans
Color separations by Chroma Graphics, Singapore
Printed and bound by Jade Productions
Production supervision by Brian G. Walker
Designed by Diane M. Earley

Can I bring my Pterodactyl to school, Ms. Johnson?

Can I?

PLEASE!?

If I brought my Pterodactyl to school
and I was playing on the monkey bars
and Butch McGurgle
climbed up next to me
and threatened to punch my lights out
if I didn't give him
my dessert
at lunch,
I wouldn't have to worry.
'Cause my Pterodactyl
would be up there
on top of Franklin Elementary.
Watching.

And he'd swoop down.
Fast.
And grab Butch McGurgle,
fly him high into the sky,
and drop him
kerplunk . . .
right in the middle
of the preschoolers' sandbox.
(My Pterodactyl would be
the BEST playground monitor. Ever!)
And Butch McGurgle would
NEVER
ask for my dessert
(or anyone else's)
at lunch
again.

Can I bring my
Pterodactyl to school,
Ms. Johnson?
Can I? PLEASE!?

If I brought my Pterodactyl to school
and our school band was on the fifty-yard line
during our homecoming game
playing our school song,
"Franklin Elementary, We Love You,"
and it started to rain
and our uniforms were beginning to get wet
and the tuba was filling up with water . . .

. . . my Pterodactyl could spread his wings.

Wide.

And cover us all.

(My Pterodactyl would be

the BIGGEST SUPER-SIZED umbrella. Ever!)

Then we could finish playing

all seven verses of

"Franklin Elementary, We Love You."

Can I bring my Pterodactyl to school, Ms. Johnson?

Can I?

PLEASE!?

If I brought my Pterodactyl to school
and there was a blizzard
and our classroom was freezing
(even though Franklin Elementary's furnace was working hard)
and we were all turning blue,
with everyone's teeth chattering nonstop,

my Pterodactyl could wrap his wings around us.
All of us.
Around you, too, Ms. Johnson.
Then we'd be comfy warm.
(My Pterodactyl would be
the COZIEST, SNUGGLIEST blanket. Ever!)
And we would NEVER have to worry
about freezing in a blizzard again.

Can I bring my Pterodactyl to school, Ms. Johnson?

Can I?

PLEASE!?

If I brought my Pterodactyl to school
on Valentine's Day,
I wouldn't have to make a valentine
for every kid in the class
like I have to do now
every year.
'Cause I could just get
a long piece of white paper
and print on it in red paint.

And my Pterodactyl could fly it
over the playground.
(My Pterodactyl would be
the HIGHEST-FLYING mail carrier. Ever!)
And all the kids in the class
could look up
and read it.
It would be the most AWESOME valentine
in the world!

Can I bring my Pterodactyl to school, Ms. Johnson?

Can I?

PLEASE!?

If I brought my Pterodactyl to school,
Mr. Rockbone,
our science teacher,
wouldn't have to take us
on a field trip to the museum
to study prehistoric animals
like he does now.

'Cause my Pterodactyl would be
Franklin Elementary's very own
Jurassic dinosaur exhibit.
(My Pterodactyl would be
the most KID-FRIENDLY dinosaur. Ever!)
And my Pterodactyl
wouldn't have signs on him saying
DO NOT TOUCH!
NO CLIMBING!
My Pterodactyl would like being touched.
And climbed on.

Can I bring my Pterodactyl to school, Ms. Johnson?

Can I?

PLEASE!?

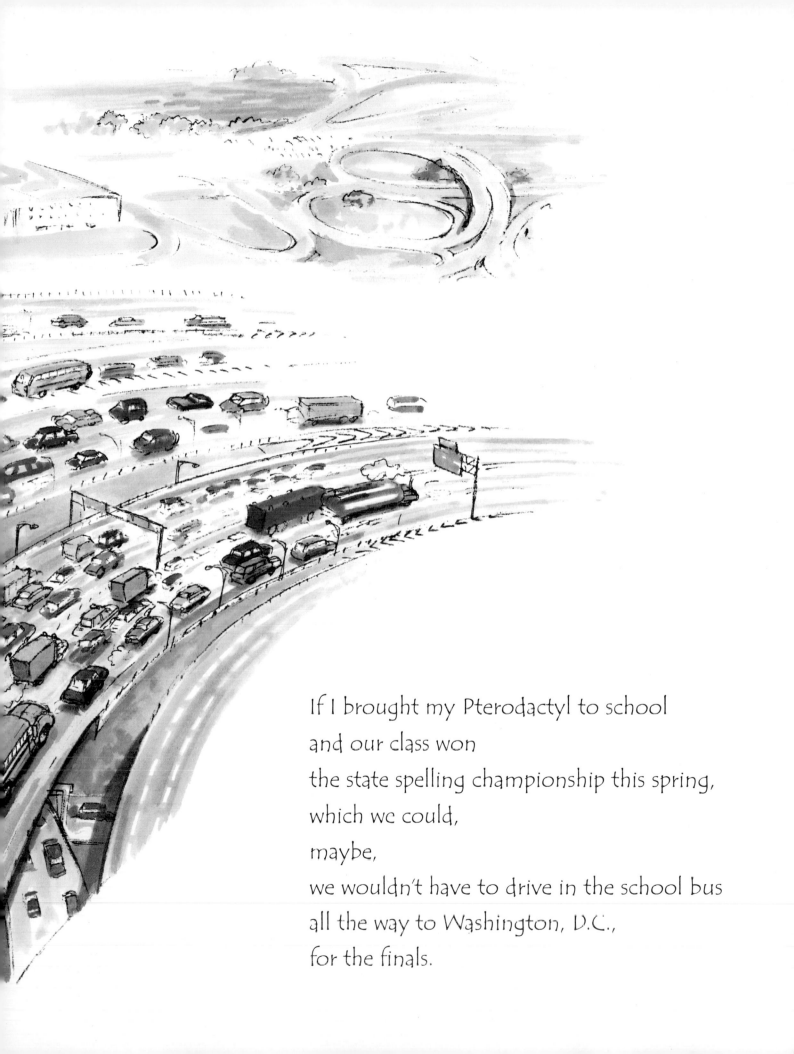

If I brought my Pterodactyl to school
and our class won
the state spelling championship this spring,
which we could,
maybe,
we wouldn't have to drive in the school bus
all the way to Washington, D.C.,
for the finals.

'Cause my Pterodactyl could fly us there.
(My Pterodactyl would make
a terrific FIRST-EVER FLYING school bus!)
Then you wouldn't have to worry
about any of us . . .
especially me . . .
turning green and getting sick
on the school bus.

If I brought my Pterodactyl to school
those last days of the school year,
right before summer vacation, when our room gets really hot,
sticky hot,
and we get really smelly,
stinky smelly
(especially after running on the playground),

my Pterodactyl could flap his wings.
Fast.
And be a giant fan.
(My Pterodactyl would be
the COOLEST fan. Ever!)
And our room would get s-o-o-o-o COOL,
we'd probably have to put on sweaters.
Maybe even mittens, too.

But Ms. Johnson,
the most IMPORTANT reason
for bringing my Pterodactyl to school—
the one that counts the MOST—
is that yesterday
I got this letter from
Unbelievable-But-True Fantastic Science Fiction magazine
saying I've won
second prize in their Win-a-Prehistoric-Animal contest.
And second prize is a Pterodactyl.
I know my mom won't let me keep a Pterodactyl
in my room unless I'm there.